Benjamin

is an Unusual Duckling

by Yann Walcker
Illustrations by Julie Mercier

AUZOU

With his turned-up beak and flowery sun hat, Benjamin really is an odd duckling! Unlike his brother and sisters, he doesn't quack… he barks!

At the barnyard, when the hens say "hello", Benjamin doesn't politely answer "Quack! Quack!" Instead, he shakes his little behind and yaps like a dog! "WOOF! WOOF! WOOF!"

At home, his parents understand that Benjamin can't help but be eccentric. He was simply born this way!

But at school, it's a different story. His classmates won't swim with him, because they think he's weird. Poor Benjamin! Look at him sitting alone on the diving board...

5

"Why don't you prove them all wrong?" suggests a wise old frog sitting at the edge of the lake. "You know, being a little different shouldn't stop you from living your life any way you want! In fact," the frog continues...

... But Benjamin is too annoyed to listen. If no one will play with him, too bad! He'd rather just leave this place. Without further ado, the duckling slips under the fence... and off he goes on what he's sure will prove to be a great adventure!

"WOOF! WOOF! WOOF!" Waddling through the ferns, Benjamin is happily yapping away. But after only a few seconds, BANG! A little mole dressed in blue overalls and wearing a helmet with a headlamp runs straight into him.

WOOF!

"Sorry Sir, I didn't seen you there!" she says, out of
breath. "My name is Marcelle. Please excuse me,
but strictly between us, I can't see a thing!"

"I am slightly visually impaired, as they say," continues Marcelle. "But don't get me wrong, I'm very good at making myself useful! Look at all these tunnels and burrows… well, I dug them myself!"

Benjamin is very impressed! Even though Marcelle can't see a thing, she sure can build beautiful homes for weasels and foxes!

As Benjamin walks away, a delicious smell tickles his nostrils. Hmmm… It's coming from a small wood cabin. The duckling picks up his pace—his mouth is watering!

Inside, a chubby rabbit named Aaron is standing in a pink apron… and he is baking a huge carrot cake. "WOOF! WOOF! WOOF! It smells so good!" barks Benjamin, his eyes wide with excitement. "May I please have a little slice?"

"I beg your pardon? What did you just say? It smells like slow-cooking mice?" asks the cook, miffed. "Stop talking nonsense and have a taste instead!"

Benjamin bursts out laughing! Despite his large ears, the rabbit is as deaf as a doorknob! But he still is an excellent chef. This cake tastes as good as it smells! Yum!

But wait, what if the frog was right? What if being different shouldn't stop you from having fun! After thanking Aaron, Benjamin takes his leave, and walks along the river…

Passing by a bale of straw, Benjamin decides
to have a little play. He gathers speed, jumps…
and comes face to face with a snake!

Terrified, the duckling starts
to shake. But, when Benjamin takes
a closer look at the reptile,
he realizes that he is not scary at all!

"Hey there!" says the snake with a very strong lisp.
"My name ith Gideon and I am a comedian!"

"When I found out that my friendth found my lithp hilariouth, I dethided to make it my career. And as I alwayth thay: my thmall flaw… is my biggetht athet!"

"WOOF! WOOF! WOOF!" laughs Benjamin. "This trip is so full of surprises! Once again, it turns out the frog was right..."

19

His feathers ruffling in the wind, Benjamin waddles through a large meadow. Suddenly, from afar, he sees a strange machine moving on its own! Intrigued, the little duckling approaches it cautiously…

But, it is not a machine! It's a big white dog! The beautiful animal named Paul is scampering along on his front paws while his hindquarters are fixed to some sort of wheelchair.

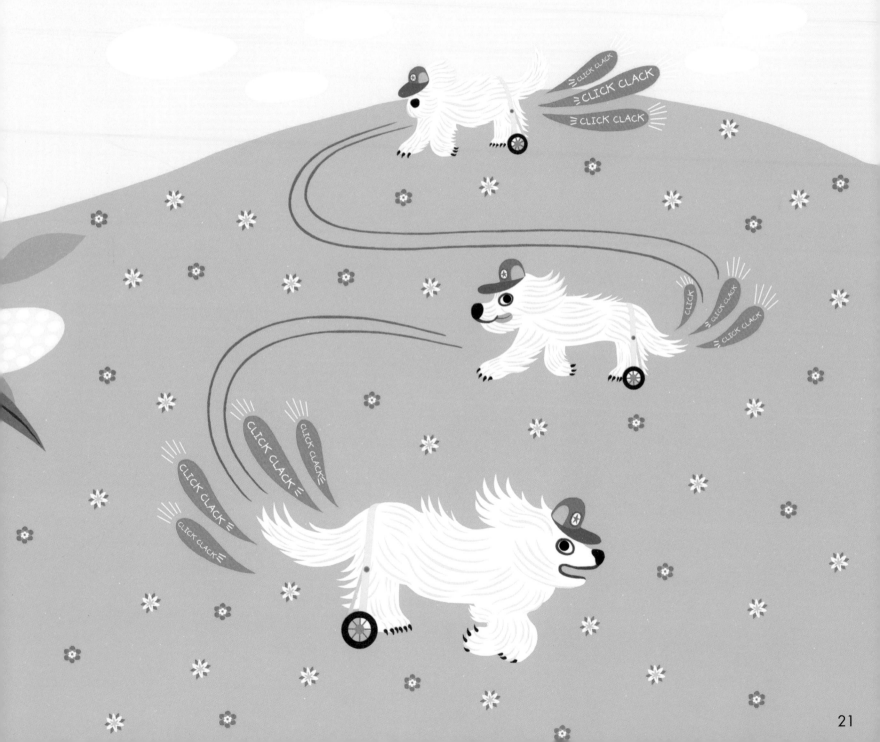

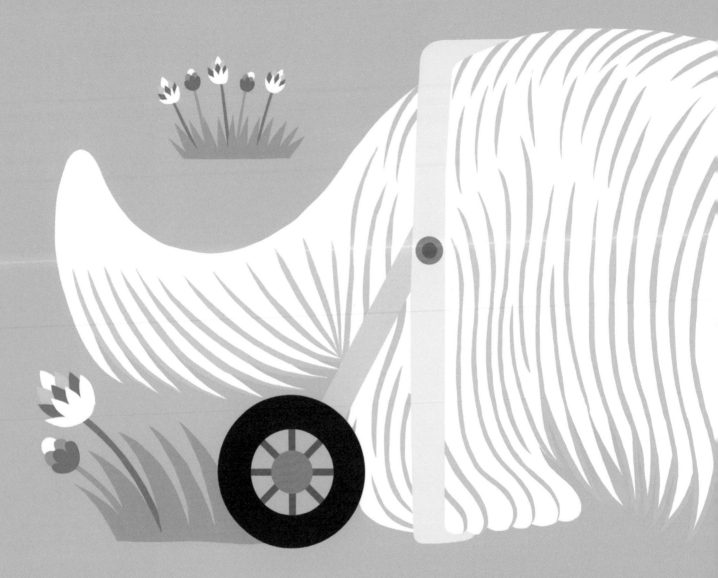

"Hi," says Benjamin, a little confused. "I... uh... What happened to you?"

"Hey! What's with the long face?" answers Paul, laughing. "I had a little accident and, since then, my hind legs just won't move. But my owner built me this cart, so I can run around again! Speaking of which, let's race each other! You'll see that I am faster than you! Yeehaaaa!"

Benjamin can't believe it. This dog is so brave!
There's no denying it, the frog was right! Paul has turned his disability
into his strength. And that's a lesson this duckling will never forget!

But right now, Benjamin needs a nap. As it happens, a pretty blackbird is sitting in the hollow of a nearby tree, with a flock of baby birds tucked under his teeny tiny wings.

"Why don't you join us?" cooes Antoine softly.

"Thank you," answers Benjamin. "But, may I ask… why aren't you flying around in the sky with all your friends?"
"Oh, that's very simple," says Antoine, smiling. "My wings are too small, I was born this way. But since I love babies, I stay here to take care of them!"

Without a sound, Benjamin settles down beside a young dove, while Antoine starts singing a lullaby. The duckling feels so good under this small yet warm wing that he falls into a deep sleep.

All of a sudden, SHBLINNG! With a start, Benjamin wakes to the sound of shattering glass. How horrible! Someone is attacking the farm! Right away, he rushes over to the house to save his friends. But what can one duckling do when faced with a dangerous robber?

SHBLINNG !

"WOOF! WOOF! WOOF!" Quick, quick, Benjamin slides under the fence…

"WOOF! WOOF! WOOF!"
He is already crossing the pond…

WOOF!
WOOF!
WOOF!

"WOOF! WOOF! WOOF!"
He is rushing to the barnyard…

WOOF!
WOOF!
WOOF!

On hearing the loud barks, the robber runs away in a panic! Benjamin can't believe it! He has managed to chase the horrible thief away. His parents are very proud of him. They hug him tightly between their wings, while his school friends, filled with admiration, now greet him like a true hero. Even the old frog applauds him.

"You see," she says, winking at him, "a dog is just fine, but there's nothing like a barking duckling to get rid of robbers!"
All the animals in the yard burst out laughing and bark with joy!
"WOOF! WOOF! WOOF!"

Managing Director: Gauthier Auzou
Editor: Claire Simon
Layout: Anne Jolly, Alice Vignaux
Production Manager: Jean-Christophe Collett
Production: Virginie Champeaud
Project Manager for the present edition: Ariane Laine-Forrest
Translation from the French: Julia Taylor
Corrector: Rebecca Frazer
Original title: Léonard est un drôle de canard

Printed in China, January 2017
ISBN: 978-2-7338-4613-1